SESAME STREET
123

Storybook ABCs

By P.J. Shaw   Illustrated by Tom Brannon

Published by Bendon Publishing International, Inc. Printed in the U.S.A.

The BENDON name and logo are trademarks of Bendon Publishing International, Inc. Ashland, OH 44805. 1-888-5-BENDON.

A
Apple

Abby, Abby, quite Cadabby,
How does your alphabet grow?
With ABC—then letters to Z!
Twenty-six, all in a row.

C
Cow

D
Dog

Cowabunga!

Hey, diddle-diddle,
The cat and the fiddle,
The cow jumped over the *moooooon*.
The little dog laughed to see such sport,
And the dish ran away with the spoon.

J
Jack

Jog and juggle! Jack, be quick!
Jack, jump over the candlestick!

Enough jogging, juggling, and jumping. I, Jack, am going back to beanstalks.

Old King Cole was a grouchy old soul,
And a grouchy old soul was he.
He called for some junk,
And he called for his skunk,
And he called his kazoo-players three.

K
King

This is kinda kooky!

L
Lamb

Prairie had a little lamb,
Little lamb, little lamb.
Prairie had a little lamb.
Its fleece was light as snow.

M
Mud

Messy Miss Muffet
Sat on a tuffet,
Eating some mud soufflé.
In marched a spider
To sit down beside her—
But she frightened that spider away!

O
Oven

P
Pie

Stop that cookie!

Oh, oh, oh! Here I go!

Pat a pie, pat a pie, baker's man.
Make me a pie as fast as you can.
Pat it and prick it and mark it with **P**.
Put it in the oven for piggy and me!

Q
Queen

Oh, I quit.

The Queen of Hearts
Made quiche and tarts,
All on a quiet day.
The Knave of Hearts,
He stole those tarts
And quickly ran away!

S
Star

Sparkle, sparkle, little star,
How I wonder what you are.
Up above the world so high,
Sprinkled in the twinkly sky.